Donald Campbell

The Caledonians and Scots

Or, the highlanders and lowlanders of Scotland. A lecture.

Donald Campbell

The Caledonians and Scots
Or, the highlanders and lowlanders of Scotland. A lecture.

ISBN/EAN: 9783337329594

Printed in Europe, USA, Canada, Australia, Japan

Cover: Foto ©Andreas Hilbeck / pixelio.de

More available books at **www.hansebooks.com**

THE

CALEDONIANS AND SCOTS;

OR,

THE HIGHLANDERS AND LOWLANDERS OF SCOTLAND.

A Lecture delivered before the Young Men's Literary and Scientific Association of Oban.

BY

D. CAMPBELL,

LATE LIEUT. 57TH REGIMENT.

EDINBURGH:

WILLIAM P. NIMMO, ST DAVID STREET.

LONDON: HOULSTON & WRIGHT, PATERNOSTER ROW.

MDCCCLXI.

EDINBURGH:
PRINTED BY ALEXANDER GRANT,
14 ST JAMES' SQUARE.

THE CALEDONIANS AND SCOTS.

MR CHAIRMAN, LADIES AND GENTLEMEN,—The history of the Highland Clans was carried down from age to age in historical poems and traditional tales, which were composed by the bards and repeated at all public gatherings by the Seannachies, two illustrious branches of the Druid order; but, unfortunately, these poems and tales seem to have been considered inaccessible by strangers, owing to the apparent difficulty of acquiring a knowledge of the Gaelic language. Hence, modern historians did not understand the patriarchal system, and were not qualified to do justice to the highland clans, even supposing that it were possible for us to presume that they were disposed to do so; but, considering the hostility which existed for ages between the highland and lowland clans, and that the historians of Scotland were all but exclusively lowlanders, it is impossible to presume that they could have been impartial. The gene-

B

ral reader has thus been so unfavourably impressed as regards the institutions and characters of the highland clans, as to render it necessary for all of you who are lowlanders or of lowland lineage to emancipate yourselves from many of your preconceived opinions before I can expect you to listen to me with impartiality; for I have opened the history of Scotland with the key of tradition, and will, very possibly, make statements calculated to stagger such of you as may not have that advantage; but I venture to say, that all intelligent readers, who can get quit of the prejudices inseparable from the perusal of partial and distorted narratives, and will attend more to the facts than to the opinions of modern historians, will find much to recommend my views of the subject, at least to a reconsideration.

The apparent difficulty of studying the Gaelic language arises from a rule which requires that the initial letter of monosyllables must be preserved in compound words. The Gaelic is a language of monosyllables; it is crowded with consonants. But, by another rule, equally simple and beautiful, the letter *h* is so managed as to shew what consonant is to be pronounced silent or aspirated. As every monosyllable or root expresses an idea, it follows that every compound Gaelic word is descriptive, instead of being a sign of the thing named, as in other languages; and the preservation of the initial letter facilitates the analysis necessary to resolve the compound words to their simple elements or roots. Had our lexicographers proceeded on this principle, instead of giving a string of arbitrary words to explain the meaning of one, every Gaelic root would have been the best interpreter of its own meaning, and Gaelic dictionaries would have furnished intrinsic and undoubted evidence of the measure of civilisation of the ancient highland clans,—thus supplying the historian and anti-quary with the means of sweeping away the cloud of contumely and misrepresentation in which ignorance and prejudice have enveloped their condi-tion and character.

The Culdees, who succeeded the Druid priesthood, were eminently evangelical. Hence, probably, their denunciation of the Druids, who professed to read, in the scheme of creation and the laws whereby nature is governed, the most convincing evidence of the existence and the will of God, as well as of the immortality of the soul; but they were evidently incapable of representing them either in their lives or their religion, otherwise they would not have adopted their names for God and the soul, as these names, from the descriptive principle on which Gaelic names are formed, express the Druid ideas on the subject, and defy misrepresentation. The title of the arch-Druid himself, for instance, was *Cobhi.* It was formed from the roots *Co*, who or what, and *bi* or *bith*, life. This title shews that biology, or the philosophy of life, was the arch-Druid's professional department in the Druid college, which was in Anglesea until destroyed by the Romans, when it was removed to Iona. The Druid's names for God and the soul also shew, so far, his progress in biology. He had three names for God—Deo, Dia, and Bith-uile. This last name is abbreviated baal or bel. *Deo* is formed from the roots *ti*, great, and *eo* or *eol*, the perfection of knowledge ; *Dia* from *ti*, great, and *agh*, good ; *Bith-uile* from *bith*, life, and *uile*, all. *D* and *t* were convertible letters, and *d* is really pronounced like the English *t*. Hence the discrepancy between the usual spelling of these compound names and their roots. We thus find that the Druid names of God represent him as the great, the perfection of knowledge, the good, the life of all. The Druid's name for the soul is *anam*, formed from the roots *an*, antagonism, defiance ; and *am*, time. That is, the antagonist or defier of time. These names, which have been adopted both by the Culdees and the translators of the Bible, thus prove that the Druid priesthood of the Celtic clans were enlightened natural theologists, and refute the calumnious statements as to their idolatry, and offering of human sacrifices. This view of the subject might be confirmed by many quotations from the ancients, but I must confine myself to the following : " The Druids," says Marcellinus, " being formed into societies or classes, devoted themselves to the study of sacred things, and maintained that the souls of men are immortal." "I should call them fools," says Diodorus Siculus, in reference to their belief in one God and the immortality of the soul, "did not Pythagorus in his cloak believe as these do in their plaids." Diogenes Laerteus describes the tenets of the Druids under four heads—to worship God, abstain from evil, exert courage, and believe in the immortality of the soul. According to highland tradition, the philanthropy and benevolence were only equalled by the energy and power of the druids. This is attested by the following among many other proverbs:

Be fagus lia ri lar,
'S faigse co'-air Co-bhi.

Close as is a flag-stone to the earth,
Closer is the succour of Covi.

The bards and seannachies, as already stated, were a separate order among the Celtic, but not the Belgic or Teutonic clans. They were the authors of their historical poems and tales, and carried them down orally from age to age. They were also the schoolmasters of the people, and itinerated among them, in shieling and clachan, instructing them orally in the poetry, music, and historical tales of their clans and country. The admirable effects of this system of tuition is visible until this day, in the morals, manners, and fireside conversation of

the remnant of the clans still left among the vales
and glens of the highlands, and in the intelligence,
sprightliness, and obliging disposition of their
children. The mission of the bard, as his name—
which is formed from the roots *bith*, life, and *ard*,
high—implies, was to improve the manners and
elevate the lives of the people by means of poetry
and music. He witnessed their conduct, and commemorated their achievements in battle, was present
at their games and sports, and complimented the
successful competitors, and was master of cere-
monies at their social and festive gatherings. The
more deeply to interest their feelings in poetry
and music, the audience were taught to join in
singing the songs both at private and public meetings. When the verse consisted of only two or
three lines, the vocalist first sung the verse, and
either the whole verse or the last line of it, was then
sung by the audience on a higher key than by the
vocalist, if a war or convivial song, and on a lower,
if a lament or love-song. When the verse consisted
of more than three lines, there was usually a chorus
combined with the song. The chorus was sung by
the audience. It was always appropriate, and studiously calculated to impart additional spirit and
pathos to the words and the melody. The company,
while singing, stood in a circle, their hands united
by means of bonnets and scarfs, which they kept
waving in accord with the time and measure of the

verses and the melody. I am convinced that this custom had the effect of interesting the hearts of the people more deeply in the *animus* both of the song and melody. Our dance-music and melodies are of unknown antiquity. There is scarcely one of our airs to which songs have been written in modern times, for which we cannot find a song, or at least a fragment of a very old song; and every one, both of our reels and strathspeys, have been carolled to humorous or satirical verses of a character sufficiently marked to instruct their own antiquity. I am of opinion that the people danced to these verses, carolled by the minstrels, before instrumental music was known. It is very much to be regretted that the traditional music, both of the highland and lowland clans, has not been published under their original names, with the snatches of humorous and satirical verses to which they were carolled by our fathers. They would, if so published, have thrown much light on the manners of the men of the olden time.

Giraldus Cambrensis was delighted with the music of Wales and Ireland. He describes the music of Ireland with enraptured and glowing eloquence; but concludes by stating that Scotland was the country to which all resorted who wished to become accomplished musicians. The music of Scotland was also described, in the days of James the First, by the Prince of Canino in a letter to a friend, as superior to that of Italy, on account of its melody. But, notwithstanding the evidence thus borne to the superior excellence of the music of Scotland at a period comparatively so remote, there are not wanting writers who deny that Scotland, or at least the highlands, ever had either poetry or music until modern times! It is, at the same time, a singular and striking peculiarity of this class of writers to express themselves only with the more arrogance, and the more self-sufficient egotism, the more ignorant they are on the subject. Thus Dr Johnson, who did not understand or pretend to understand Gaelic, and who, therefore, must necessarily have been totally ignorant of Gaelic literature, describes that language as the rude gibberish of a barbarous people, who, as they conceived grossly, were contented to be grossly understood; and Sir James Macintosh and Lord Macaulay spoke in at least equal ignorance of the subject, and in a spirit equally coarse and presumptuous.

The Rev. Mr Macdonald, and Messrs Gow, Marshall, &c., &c., have credit with most writers for the authorship of the melodies, reels, and strathspeys which they published; and, having given them new names, in compliment to their patrons, without any explanation, it would seem as if they had no objection to take credit for the composition of them. At the same time, I am myself convinced that they never meant to convey such an idea, and had given these new names without being alive to, or conscious of the natural inference to be drawn from the circumstance. But be that as it may, every one of the melodies, reels, and strathspeys copied and published by these gentlemen were, and still are, floating traditionally through the vales and glens of the highlands; but we owe them a deep debt of gratitude for having rescued so many of them from obscurity. I cannot, however, help remarking that, depriving the music of the air and signet of antiquity belonging to these old names, in servile laudation of their patrons and patronesses, was anything but in good taste.

I am of opinion that much of the music of Scotland has only received its national spirit and expression from the genius of the country. I differ entirely from those who associate barbarity with antiquity, and have no doubt that comparative philology, which I hope soon to see established as a science, will prove that much of all the arts of civilisation, as well as much of the music of Europe, had been carried, by the earliest colonies, from the east. I have myself heard highland music among the peasantry on both sides of the Pyrenees; and it was only the other day that I recognised, in the song to which Russian seamen were discharging timber at Leith, the old sea ditty, beginning

Ho! se mo run a maraich, &c.

The seannachi, whose name is derived from the

roots *sean*, old, and *chi*, to see (into "the days of other years") also itinerated among the people, reciting and illustrating their historical tales and poems. These historical tales, of which the bards and seannachies were the authors, were rendered powerful in their impression on the hearts of the people by a happy combination of poetic simile and metaphor, and by all the charms of the most chaste and lively style, and the most striking and graceful elocution. Although the history of their own country and clans formed the chief subject of these traditional poems and tales, yet many of them, especially of the tales, were founded on the adventures of the wild and daring Northmen, not only in Britain and Ireland, but also in France, Italy, and Greece. When a party of savans, commissioned by the King of Sweden, were travelling through Scotland, in search of ancient monuments connected with the achievements of these chivalrous but rapacious warriors a few years ago, I regretted much that the collection of these fast-disappearing tales did not form a prominent object of the mission. I have heard scores of these tales in my younger days, and wish every success to Mr Campbell (of Islay), who has taken on himself the mission of collecting and publishing any remnants of them that may still be extant in the highlands and isles.

The system of tuition by oral lectures, and the residence of the same clans in the same districts

from age to age, whereby an enlightened public
opinion was concentrated as a check on corruption or
innovation—together with the well-known integrity
of the bards and seannachies themselves—afford a
sufficient assurance that these historical poems and
tales were carried down in all their native purity
and integrity during the period of their existence
as an order. But, unfortunately for Gaelic literature,
when the kings of Scotland succeeded to the throne
of England, owing to *ultra vires* grants of land by
feudal charters (the object of which I will by
and by explain), the bards and seannachies,
defrauded of the estates secured to them by the
custom or *cleachda* of former ages, ceased to exist
as an order, and became mere wanderers, living on
the hospitality of the people. This was the most
fatal blow struck not only at the literature, but
also at all the rights and privileges of the clans, of
which the bards and seannachies were the vigilant
and stern guardians—for, although many penal
statutes were enacted against them, on that account,
by the feudal kings of the Scots and their creatures,
they failed to put down or lessen the influence of
the order, until defrauded of their estates, and ejected
and dispersed.

The Celtic clans of Scotland and Ireland preserved
the patriarchal system, and lived in a state of
disunited independence, under their local clan
governments, to a much later period than the general

reader is aware of. Every clan elected its own government, consisting of a judge, called *Breidheadh*, modernised Brehon ; an executive, called *Maor-mor*, modernised chief; and a jury, composed of the *ceann-ta'ighs*—that is, the heads of the different houses or branches of the clan-modernised chieftains. The chief or executive was not a member of the *Mōd*, which is called the Brehon court in Ireland and Wales, where the record of its laws and proceedings have been much better preserved than in Scotland. The Brehon laws were carried down orally from age to age, and, being equally simple and equitable, were understood and appreciated by the people. They were the only laws ever recognised or obeyed by the clans. Indeed, the feudal enactments, now dignified by the name of Acts of Parliament, were never known to nor obeyed by the people beyond the immediate neighbourhood of the court. The feudal nobility neither knew nor administered any other laws than their own will and pleasure ; the magistrates of the free burghs had and administered only their own municipal laws; and the clans adhered firmly to their *cleachda* or custom—as the Brehon laws were termed. The enactment of these so-called laws amused the kings and their creatures, but fell still-born from the pen. Their resuscitation, dry-nursing, and adolescence, was the work of the modern lawyer. All cases competent to be brought and tried before the Brehon court admitted of being compensated by an *eric*, which is an abbreviation of *adhairc*, horns, the compensation being paid in horned sheep and cattle.*

TRANSLATION BY O'DONOVAN.

* "The right of Caiseal and of the king of Caiseal from [his] territories generally down here.

With the Musraidhe, in the first place, this tribute begins, *i.e.* ten hundred cows and ten hundred hogs from the Musraidhe.

A hundred cows, and a hundred pigs, and a hundred oxen from the men of Uaithne.

Two hundred wethers, and a hundred hogs, and a hundred cows, and a hundred green mantles from the men of Ara.

A hundred cows, and a hundred oxen, and a hundred hogs from Corca Laighe.

Ten hundred oxen and ten hundred cows from Corca Dhuibhne also.

Ten hundred cows and ten hundred hogs from Ciarraidhe Luachra.

Ten hundred cows and ten hundred oxen from Corca Bhais-cainn.

A thousand cows, and a thousand oxen, and a thousand rams, and a thousand cloaks from Boirinn.

A hundred cows, and a hundred oxen, and a hundred sows from Seachtmbodh.

Two thousand hogs and a thousand cows from the Deise.

It is not for inferiority [of race] that they pay these tributes, but for their territories, and for the superiority of the right of Caiseal, and for its having been blessed by Patrick as Benean sung."

THE RIGHT OF TEMORA AND THE CHIEFS OF TEMORA.

"Cisadin acus besa rig Teamrach o thuathaib and so, feib ro ernet acus ro icaid fri cond acus fri cormac acus fri Cairppi, conid dib gabsad rigi iar suidin. Cemeas cana acus com-ica cean Tormach ar daig saidbri, cean earnam ar dai bri act mina theagaim dith for

Cases deemed capital were transferred to the Druid court, as the Celtic clans held that life could not lawfully be taken away (unless in a fair duel or battle) excepting by the recognised servants of the

finib no plaig no una no dumbath, a thobach, iar-coimead acus iar-comlaigead m cach bliadain."

Note.—The above is pure Gaelic; but sadly deformed by the spelling.—D. C.

TRANSLATION BY O'DONOVAN.

"The rents and the customs and the refections of the king of Tiamhair from his CHIEFTAINS [thuathaib] here, as they yielded and paid them to Conn and to Cormac and to Cairbre, from whom (*i.e.* from whose race) they subsequently selected kings. The tribute and the payment must be the same [at all times] without any addition for increased wealthiness, without deficiency for impoverishment, unless in case of a destruction of the tribe, or plague, or famine, or mortality—to be levied, be it great or be it little every year.

Note.—The foregoing extracts from the valuable works edited for learned societies in Ireland, by John O'Donovan, Esq., M.R.I.A., barrister at law, Dublin, shews a marked distinction between the southern and northern clans of Ireland. The so-called Gothic clans paid their tribute directly to the King of Caiseil, *but not in sign of inferiority of race.* To understand why this remark is made in LEABHAR-NAN-CEART, pronounced léh-vár-nan kèrt, the statement made elsewhere must be remembered, namely, that every tribe in succession furnished the Ceann-Cath, pronounced Kén-Káh or war-chief, who took the title of King of Caisel, and that his tribe, being the ruling tribe for the time, paid no tribute. Hence, to guard against the assumption that the tribute was paid in token of subjection, the other clans paid, as it were, under the above protest, regularly recorded in the book of rights. But the marked distinction to which I wish to call attention is, that the Gothic great and good Being by whom life is given. Hence, when the Druids were superseded by the Culdees, capital punishments ceased among the patriarchal clans, and were only known among the feudal

clans paid their tribute directly to the king, who paid their *tuarasdal*, pronounced too-ar-as-tall, literally wages, to the inferior chiefs, who were thus stamped as his hired servants ; while the Celtic clans paid their tribute directly to their own elected chiefs, and the chiefs paid the Ceann-Cath, or King of Temora for the time —thus preserving in appearance, as well as in fact, the dependance of the chiefs on the support of the people, and the dependance of the king on the support of the chiefs.

It is thus shewn by Leabhar-nan-ceart, that, although the Gothic clans had fixed tenures, they held their lands from the king, and paid their tribute in acknowledgment of " the superiority of the right of Caisel." The Celtic clans, on the contrary, admitted no superior over the lands of the clan. Their chiefs were elected, and they supported them by a voluntarily fixed tribute ; and the chiefs elected the ceann-cath or king, and supported him by a voluntarily fixed tribute also.

When the kings of the Scots adopted the feudal system, there are sufficient grounds for believing that the object of the charters granted over the lands of the clans was to give the king the same power over the Caledonian chiefs which he had over the Scottish chiefs. This was not attainable under the patriarchal system ; consequently the servitude imposed on the chiefs, by these charters, were personal to themselves and their heirs. No new servitude is imposed on the clans in these charters. On the contrary, they, in the general case bear *ex facie* to be "confirmations" of immemorial rights, derived from the *cleachda* or custom, and almost always contain a clause to the effect that the clans were to continue in the performance of the services which were incumbent on them under the cleachda or custom of their ancestors. No chief pretended to be the proprietor of the soil in right of these charters, or presumed that he had a right to increase the calpa or fixed number of young followers of lords or barons whose charters contained powers of pit and gallows, or at the king's justice-aires—the Culdees having declined to act as criminal judges, or to interfere in any shape with secular matters. Parties guilty of crimes, punishable by death, were tried before the Brehon court, and if found guilty, deprived of their names, and all clan rights and privileges, and banished. When the crime was not treacherous or infamous, these banished men generally received an asylum from some distant clan ; but when their crimes were treacherous or infamous, the banished men took shelter in the caves and wilds of the country, and lived, as they best could, under the general name of *cearnaich coille*, or warriors of the woods. The

stock, payable by the clans, until after the union with England. The effect given to feudal charters in England then began to be, l it by bit, extended over the clans of Scotland, until the people of the lowlands first, and then the people of the highlands, ꞏwere defrauded of their fixed tenures, by an insidious usurpation, and ejected from their native districts or expatriated. Duncan ban Macintyre, in his poem of *Coire gorm an fhasich*, pronounced Kōh-réé kórm an āh-*sééch* (guttural) only repeated, substantially, and in the same tender and pathetic manner, the melancholy dirge over the desolation of his country, which was sung by Burn, the border minstrel, some century before him ; and the enactments, by the kings of the Scots and their creatures, which modern lawyers dignify by the name of Acts of Parliament, shew that the kings regarded these charters as mere superiorities, which they could recall at pleasure. Half the superiorities granted down to that date were thus recalled and annexed to the crown by Act of Parliament, 41, anno 1455.—D.C.

former of these classes often attained great distinction among their adopted clans by heroism and fidelity. They are honourably represented by the Clan Glassarich of Braelochaber, and the Clan Uaric or Rory of Lochiel and Glengary ; and the *cearnaich coille* are characteristically represented in *Waverley* by Donald Bane Lean.

Sir Walter Scott, in the *Fair Maid of Perth*, describes the ceremonial of inaugurating a chief, but very imperfectly.   He did not understand the difference between the feudal and patriarchal systems of government. The best feudal writer on the tenures and elective privileges of the clans is Spenser, who enters fully into the subject in a small and rare book, which he published in London, on his return from Ireland, in the reign of Queen Elizabeth. Yet even Spenser did not well understand the laws and rights of the Celtic clans, for he thought that capital crimes could be, and sometimes were, compromised before the Brehon court.   On the contrary, the court had no discretionary power, its laws being unalterable, and the crimes and their penalties both classed and fixed.   He also conceived that the Irish having agreed, in a treaty with the viceroy of England, Anthony St Leger, to make King Henry the sovereign of Ireland, had thereby become bound to obey his laws, although he himself acknowledges that they had, in the treaty, reserved all their former rights and privileges (which surely included

their own laws) inviolate. The Irish denied to
Spenser that their fathers had agreed to confer on
Henry any greater power than was possessed by
their native king, who was neither the fountain of
honour, the proprietor of the soil, nor the source of
laws and jurisdictions, as in England.   He tells
us that they obstinately adhered to their elective
privileges and Brehon courts, which accordingly
exercised their usual jurisdiction in every district
in Ireland, excepting the small circle, called the
pale, occupied by the English.   The Irish farther
contended that their ancestors could not prejudice
them in their tenures, having no estate in any of
their lands, signiories, or hereditaments longer than
during their own lives—because "all the Irish held
their lands by *tainistry*, which is no more than a
personal estate during his life-time, that is, *tainist*,
by reason that he is admitted thereunto by election
of the country."

The *tainister*, who was always appointed on the
election of every new chief, represented the clan
in their tenures and civil rights, and was the
special guardian of both.   Spenser states that it
was the custom among the Irish "presently after the
death of one of their chief lords or captains, to
assemble into a place generally appointed and known
to them, to choose another in his place, when they
do, for the most part, nominate and elect, not the
eldest son, nor any of the children of the lord

deceased, but the next to him of blood, as commonly the next brother unto him—if he have any—or the next cousin, or so forth, as any is elder or worthier in that kin or sept;" "and next unto him do they choose a tainister, who shall succeed unto him should he live thereunto.". "I have heard," continues Spenser, "that the beginning and cause of this ordinance was specially for the defence and maintenance of the lands in their pastority, and for excluding all innovation or alienation thereof to strangers. Hence they say, as erst I told you, that they reserved their titles, signiories, and tenures sound and whole to themselves."

The above is clear and explicit, and can leave no doubt that the king and government of the British empire, in changing the laws and tenures of the people of Ireland, had violated the treaty whereby the sovereignty of Ireland was conferred on the king of England. The assumption that Ireland has been conquered by England, in the face of the treaty with Anthony St Leger, recognised by so high an authority as Spenser, and many other well-known treaties, and especially innumerable letters of black mail, granted (for protection) from time to time, by the lords of the *pale* to the patriarchal chiefs of Ireland, is simply ridiculous. The wars of England in Ireland never professed nor assumed the magnitude of a conquest. The pale was the wages received by Strongbow for restoring the banished and

infamous M'Murrough, and the object of the English
expeditions was to maintain and defend the possession of it. It was the colonisation of Ulster by the
Scottish Solomon that struck at the root of the
patriarchal institutions of Ireland, and not the arms
of England. The same dynasty—the Scoto-Irish
dynasty—thus it was which, in reality, defrauded
the clans both of Scotland and Ireland, not only of
their immemorial title in the soil of their native
land, but also of their equitable Brehon laws, and the
elective rights and privileges which they inherited,
under the patriarchal institutions, both of their
Celtic and Belgic ancestors. The much abused
Anglo-Saxons (if they be really anything else than
a myth) are certainly guiltless of the conquest or
oppression either of the Irish or any other people.
The writers who ascribe to the misnamed Anglo-
Saxons the English wars in France, Wales, Ireland,
and Scotland, forget that England was conquered
by the Normans, who reduced the people into serfs,
and did not allow them to carry arms until the
period of the revolution. England owes to her
Anglo-Norman conquerors (not the so-called Anglo-
Saxons) every military achievement of which she can
boast until her union with Scotland and Ireland.

Land tenures, by feudal grants from the crown,
were unknown in England until the conquest, and in
Scotland until subsequently to the reign of Malcolm
Ceann-mor. Now, as the Scottish monarchy existed

for ages before the date of these charters, the people must have held the lands on some competent title—such as the patriarchal *cleachda* or custom—for time immemorial. It does not, therefore, seem either unreasonable or unimportant to inquire by what means the people lost, and the king acquired, the property of the soil of Scotland. Sir Walter Scott, in the *Tales of a Grandfather*, mentions a tradition to the effect that the people had surrendered their inherent right in the soil to the king, and infefted him therein in due feudal form by delivering to him earth and stone. Sir Walter adds, as corroborative of the tradition, that the Moothill of Scone is made up of these symbols of surrender and infeftment, and therefore called *omnis terra*. The tradition proves one thing very clearly, namely, that the soil, according to the common belief of former ages, belonged to the people in common (*omnis terra*), and that the king could only acquire a legal title to the soil through their consent and surrender. Were an action of declarator of the legality and intended effect of feudal charters brought before the Court of Session, by a competent party, I greatly question whether the result would prove satisfactory to the clearance-makers, the Moothill of Scone notwithstanding, unless prescription applies to *ultra vires* charters, and *mala fide* possessions. At any rate, the people of Scotland might say, as the people of Ireland said to Spenser, that their ancestors had no estate in the lands excepting during their own lives ; and therefore that they could not, by any act of theirs, prejudice the right of their descendants to the soil, that right being the inherent and vital principle of the patriarchal or clan system. But, indeed, it can be shewn historically, as well as by those edicts of the kings of the Scots and their creatures, which are now being respected as legitimate Acts of Parliament, that the object of these charters was to substitute the feudal for the patriarchal organisation and discipline of the people. It was never intended by the kings that these charters should carry to the grantees the property of the soil, but simply the superiority held by the elected tainist, and the *calpa*, or fixed number of young cattle, payable by the clans to their officials. It never was meant that these charters, which, in so far as native chiefs and chieftains were the recipients, are, with very rare exceptions, mere confirmations of unwritten and immemorial rights, should empower the grantees to eject the people, or alter their immemorially fixed rents ; and, in point of fact, no such power or claim was exercised on the plea of these charters until the clan organisation, and the power of combined action resulting from it, ceased to exist. This disruption was a natural and legitimate consequence of the union with England, the permanent establishment of peaceful relationships between the two countries, and the total change in the habits and pursuits of both peoples ; but the House of the Commons of England, knowing that the people of Scotland were not represented there, ought to have watched over their interest, and to have prevented the confiscation, in effect, of their right in common, to the soil of their native land, from being also a consequence of the union. That these charters were not meant as grants of the property of the soil, is farther proved by the fact, that the kings considered themselves at liberty to cancel, recall, or transfer the superiorities carried by them at pleasure, and that there is abundant evidence of their having frequently done so. The following enactment by James the First, which I quote verbatim, also proves that no change in the ownership or possession of the soil had resulted from these charters down to that date ; or, in other words, that every labouring man then in Scotland was a "portioner" in the soil of his native land. This act is entitled an act "anent men quha suld labour the land."

"Item. It is ordained that ilk man of simple estaite, that suld be by reason labourers, have auther halfe ane oxe in the pleuch, or else delve ilk day seven fute of length and seven on breadhth, under the painc of ane oxe to the king."

Now, it will not, I think, be argued that this enactment embraced men who had no land and no oxen. Yet it embraces every labouring man in Scotland in the reign of James the First—"every man that suld be by reason labourers."

Clanships were communities of brothers and sisters. This is implied by their name of *clann*, children —that is, children of the patriarch or founder of the tribe. The chief was, therefore, elected, not on the principle of his being heir to the last chief, but on the principle of his being the nearest in descent to the common ancestor and founder of the clan ; and, consequently, his living representative, and, as such, the father of the clan. The chieftains, or heads of the different branches of the clan, were elected by their respective families of the clan on the same principle. Richard of Cirencester, on account of this custom, describes the ancient Briton clans as democracies resembling aristocracies. They were democracies, because the property of the lands, and the power of electing their own rulers, were vested in the people ; and they were aristocracies, because purity of blood, and nobility of descent from the common ancestor or founder of the clan, were the only conditions of aristocracy that could be recognised by a people whose king was not the fountain of honour, but merely the ceann-cath, or war-chief. All clan rights and privileges were held to have been derived from the whole clan or children in common from the common ancestor. Hence the reason why the chief was elected on the principle of being the nearest link in the chain of clan-descent to the common ancestor or founder of the tribe. This is what is called tainistry in Scotland, Ireland, and Wales. The word is formed from the roots *teannas,* nearest, and *air,* HIM, the common ancestor. The chief, after his election, was regarded as representing the patriarch or founder, and, therefore, as the father of the clan. He then ceased to be styled *tainister,* and that title was bestowed formally on his apparent successor, who was elected at the same time, and who represented the clan in their tenures and civil rights. Owing to this rule of succession, the brother usually succeeded to the brother, and the nephew to the uncle, instead of the son succeeding to the father, as in the feudal succession. No person, therefore, who did not recognise all rights and honours derived from the common ancestor as the inheritance, equally and in common of the whole clan, would be elected as chief, or *tainister ;* and I could quote many cases in which tainisters were passed over in the election, and chiefs deposed after election, for a violation or attempted violation of this principle of clanships. But modern chiefs or chieftains do not know, or seem to forget this peculiarity in clanships. Yet it was this peculiarity that constituted the very soul of the system—namely, the perfect unity and equality of the whole clan, in blood, in pedigree, in tenures, in political power, and every clan right and privilege. The whole clan was responsible for and bound to pay the *eric* discerned against every individual clansman failing his own means, and every individual clansman was liable for the whole clan, not only according to the Brehon laws, but also according to the feudal enactments that sought to break up the clan system. Hence the feudal custom, mentioned in various edicts, of making clans put some of their number in ward as pledges for clan engagements. But modern highland gentlemen, unaccustomed to discriminate between the peoples of the different parts of the empire (though that difference is still not only discernible, but striking), while trying to restore ancient games and customs, forget the broad distinction between the patriarchal and feudal systems. Gradations of rank, from the king downwards, every class having despotic power over their inferiors, were the characteristics of feudalism. This iron despotism was exercised by the higher over the lower ranks in civil as well as military matters. The clans, on the contrary, like the modern volunteers, elected their officers out of their own ranks, and allowed them no discretionary power either in civil or military matters—every officer, as well as every other member of the clan being bound to conform to the *cleachda*, or custom, and amenable to the Brehon court. From ignorance, apparently, of this broad distinction between the free clansman of the patriarchal and the bond vassal or serf of feudalism, these gentlemen do not seem to see

anything inconsistent with the spirit of the patriarchal system in holding meetings to celebrate the
manly games of their ancestors under the protection
or patronage of some titled personage. I certainly
have no prejudice against dukes, lords, or baronets ;
and admit that a fiddler or cobbler on the tramp,
especially in the palmy days of feudalism, might
humbly petition for their patronage, with the view
of being allowed to fiddle or cobble among their
retainers for his bread, without any excess of servility ;
but I cannot regard it otherwise than utterly
inconsistent with the spirit of our highland ancestors,
to see plaided and bonneted bands of armed and
warlike highlanders celebrating their games under
patronage. The "keep aye booing" propensity,
which gained an unenviable notoriety for a
" M'Sycophant" and a " M'Whabble," was at one
time supposed to be characteristic of feudal flunky-
ism ; but more than one of my lowland literary
friends are now beginning to associate excessive
politeness with the kilt—or at least with the directors
of highland societies—a most unnatural association !

The fulsome pretensions of a highland chief, who
was known to Sir Walter Scott, and the considerate
forbearance, or, perhaps, the servile acquiescence of
his followers, was the cause, in all probability, of
the very erroneous views of clanships formed by the
great Scottish novelist. Hence · the saline boundary
which he draws between the clan and their officials

at the table of Vic Ivor vic Ian Vohr; but had
Sir Walter qualified himself to write on the subject,
by making acquaintance with the poetry and traditions of the clans, he would have drawn a very
different picture. In the preface to Macdonald's
Collection of Gaelic Poetry, of which he could have
found a copy in the Advocates' Library, he might
have seen that no such exhibition of serfishness
could take place among clansmen. It was the
custom for the seannachies to stand at the entrance,
on every occasion of a festive gathering among the
clans, to remind them of their perfect equality one
with another. This equality he proclaimed in the
words of which the following is a translation :
"Sit turner, sit tailor, sit every man in the readiest
place, and sit thou arrow-maker." And, to render
it impossible for any one to arrogate to himself any
position above another, they always sat in a circle, so
that the round table was neither fabulous nor peculiar
to King Arthur, but the regular rule at every Celtic
banquet. It is only since the clan system was
broken up that a spurious species of feudal pride,
affected by the ignorant and insignificant among the
highland *lairds,* occasionally supplanted the dignity
and courtesy of the native manners. I am satisfied
that he would not long be tolerated as a chief that
would dare to shew an indignity or discourtesy to
his clan, while clanships were something else than
a mere theme for the creative genius of the novelist.

Every clansman was by birth a gentleman, according to the highland *cleachda* or custom, and was always treated, in every clan district, with the consideration due to a gentleman ; and such was the effect on their character of this beautiful feature in the clan system, that there are few highlanders known to tradition who failed to conduct themselves on all occasions, and sometimes even under the most adverse circumstances, in accordance with what was considered faithful and honourable in their own age and country. It has become too much the custom of the English-speaking public to judge of the peoples of the different parts of the empire by the present standard of right and wrong in England, and to blame the highlanders, Welsh and Irish, not unfrequently in ignorance of the injustice by which the acts they condemn were provoked, or the motives by which the assumed delinquents were actuated. The different peoples of the different parts of the empire ought to be judged by the circumstances in which they were placed, and the standard of right and wrong in their own country and age. That standard, among the highland clans, though very different, can well bear to be compared to the standard of right and wrong in the feudal ages of England ; and the conduct of the clans, under circumstances of usurpation and oppression on the part of the king and nobility of Scotland, was bold, lofty, and determined, yet humane, forbearing, and considerate. But history does them anything but justice, chiefly for the reason already stated. The fact is, from the date of the usurpation of feudal power by our kings, Scotland has been governed in effect by civil wars, treacherously fomented by the feudal clans, from time to time, for the purpose of substituting the feudal despotism introduced into England by the Norman conquerors, for the free and elective custom of their native land. The patriarchal clans resisted this usurpation, and refused to accept feudal charters. Then the kings, equally determined and unscrupulous, fell upon ways and means to provoke clan after clan into acts of resistance that might plausibly be construed into rebellion. Warrants of fire and sword were then issued, first against the more weak and isolated clans, but by degrees against the most powerful ; and such of the feudal lords already established in the country, as could muster a sufficient number of vassals, were set loose on the prey. However weak or unprepared a clan might be, it never refused battle ; but the result usually was their reduction into the state emphatically denounced as "broken clans" in feudal enactments. This condition was tantamount to being outlawed. Their lands were then assumed to have been forfeited, and the superiority of them was transferred, by feudal charters, to one or other of the minions—usually foreigners—of the crown. I could mention many clans who had been thus studiously goaded or entrapped into a construed treason or rebellion, and whose lands fell to the favourites or creatures of the king ; but the fate of the high-minded and generous Clan Gregor is well known, and may suffice as an example.

I have remarked elsewhere on the hostility which existed for ages between the highlanders and low-landers, and on the ignorance and prejudices of modern historians as regards the institutions and character of the highland clans. In reading the history of Scotland, it is thus necessary, if truth be our object, to make a broad distinction between the facts stated by our historians, and their opinions and inferences in reference to the highland clans. For instance, if we take the facts stated in the histories of Wallace and Bruce, apart from the strictures of historians, we will find that the lowland clans never made any effectual stand against the invader under these heroic leaders. This is accounted for by the fact that a very considerable part of the lowlands was under the influence of feudal lords, who placed more value on lands and titles than on the independence of Scotland. But we ought not to forget that these feudal lords were chiefly, if not all, of foreign extraction ; and that a powerful feudal sovereign, having a country and a people to divide among his followers, was not very likely to be, to such adventurers, an object of hostility. The Scottish nobility of the age of Bruce and Wallace were some of them the invaders' most subtile and treacherous spies, and some of them his most wise and distinguished generals. It is not, therefore, so much to be wondered at that the lowlanders never fought a battle worthy of the name against the invader under Wallace or Bruce; but on every disaster or defeat in the lowlands, these heroes, with their more faithful and devoted followers, fled beyond the friths or the Grampians, where they never failed to find not only a secure asylum, but also an army, by whose trenchant claymores, and unyielding patriotism and pluck, their disasters were retrieved and the independence of the country ultimately secured. The battle of Stirling was gained by Wallace with men collected beyond the friths; and two-thirds of the men of Bannockburn were highlanders. Hence Burns, who knew the traditions as well as the history of his country, designates the men who fought the battle of Stirling as "Caledonians;" and Tytler shews that the lowland nobility and their vassals had joined the invader, and fought against Wallace at Stirling. These are not matters of opinion, but facts which defy contradiction. Yet those who will follow the narratives of historians, without detecting the latent facts glossed over in them, will give credit to the lowland clans for the successful stand made against the invader, and regard the country beyond the friths, which supplied the men of the battle of Stirling as a *terra incognita*, occupied only by a few roving clans, who picked up a precarious and miserable subsistence by making forays on the few honest families of Saxon squatters scattered over the border of the highlands.   And so much are we the creatures of first impressions, as to make it difficult for us, even in our mature years, to get quit of the impression made on our minds at school by the works of historians whose every paragraph, in so far as the highlanders are concerned, convicts them of ignorance and prejudice.   Than the highlands, when under the management of the officials, elected by the clans, and under fixed tenures and rents, no country could have been better adapted to the support of a great warlike rural population ; and there is in fact no country which shews more extensive traces on shores, straths, vales, glens, and even wolds of the great agricultural enterprise and industry of unknown ages ; yet I venture to say, that not one in a thousand, not only of the intelligent English tourists who visit the country annually, but even of the native lowlanders, have made these traces a subject of research and contemplation, or who deplore the miserable infatuation and mismanagement by which a fertile and salubrious country has been laid desolate, and a virtuous and warlike people defrauded of their undoubted right to the soil of their native land, and expatriated.   This want of sympathy with the highlanders, under the injustice and oppression to which they have been

D

subjected, is to be ascribed to preconceived opinions derived from works, which, in so far as the highlanders are concerned, are less truthful than any of our novels.

Such, gentlemen, is the true explanation of the feuds and rebellions charged upon the highland clans. They were, without exception, the result of treacherous schemes, concocted by the Stuart kings and their creatures for the purpose of goading or inveigling the clans into acts of construed treason or rebellion—and so insuring their subjection to feudalism or their extirpation. The memorable address of the nobility, &c., of Scotland, to the Pope against the first Edward, remarks on the peaceful character and uniform unanimity of the clans among themselves down to that age; and I defy any man to point out a clan "*feud*" or battle which did not originate (as the very name feud, by which they are known, implies) in some of these iniquitous charters, granted to one party over the property immemorially belonging to another. The kings of Scotland were, in effect, down to the period of feudalism, merely the war-chiefs of the clans. Their assumption of despotic power, and the property of the soil, were therefore purely acts of usurpation; therefore their grants of feudal superiorities over the lands of the people are *ultra vires*. The clans resisted them as illegal, and sure I am, that had the people of England been similarly situated, and acted in a similar manner, instead of being condemned, that their conduct would not only meet with approval, but also with commendation from every enlightened and liberal writer at this day in England. When a history of Scotland, worthy of the name, shall have been published, the people of England and the lowlands will regard the long calumniated and much misrepresented highland clans as one of the noblest families of the human race.

Bruce, although that fact is scarcely explained by Scottish historians, claimed the crown on the patriarchal principle of succession, namely, on the ground of his being a step nearer in descent than Baliol to the founder of the dynasty ; and he contended that this was in accordance with the law and practice in Scotland. Baliol, on the other hand, claimed on the feudal principle of direct legal descent ; and pled that since the king of the Scots succeeded to the throne of the Picts, such was both the law and practice in Scotland. Hence the highland clans sided with Bruce, and the lowland clans with Baliol. Nevertheless, Bruce's first step, on finding himself king, was to secure the succession, by an Act of Parliament, in his own lineal descendants. This was a fatal blow to the peculiar principle of succession of the highland clans—for, from that date, the chiefs and chieftains, like the king, became unfaithful to the *cleachda* or custom, and never rested until the succession was also made hereditary in their descendants. The clans, however, must have been gradually won over to the change—at least, it is difficult on any other supposition to understand how the patronymics by which the chiefs and chieftains have since then been distinguished could have been assumed permanently.

But although the office of chief and chieftain had thus become hereditary, the clans still adhered to the ceremonial and the oath of inauguration of every new chief. As already stated, the ceremonial of installation or inauguration is described by Sir Walter Scott in the *Fair Maid of Perth;* but Spenser describes both the ceremonial and the oath more fully and accurately in the work to which I have already referred. The ceremonial and the oath were no doubt the same in all clan countries ; yet, I have not heard that the oath emitted by the highland chiefs imposed any other obligation than the maintenance inviolate, during their lifetime, of all the former rights and privileges of the clan. But in Ireland, according to Spenser, the chief, in addition to the above, made oath that he would give up the chiefship peacefully to his tainist whenever required to do so by the clan.

Bruce called, what is absurdly enough designated a meeting of heritors, seeing that the soil belonged to the whole people in common. The chiefs and chieftains who attended the meeting, being called on to shew the titles by which they held their lands, drew their swords, and presented them, point fore-most, to the king.   Bruce was awed by an act so spontaneous and significant, and never again called for a sight of clan tenures ; yet that crafty monarch, and his successors, contrived to cover the country with clandestinely issued and received charters.   These charters, in so far as the highland clans were concerned, remained a profound secret until the clan system was broken up by the disasters of Culloden.   Some of them have since then stepped into light, and been made available at the points of the bayonets of a standing army.

We have thus seen that the king of Scotland had no civil jurisdiction, and that his military power was limited to the time of war.   Nay, more.   The clans were only bound to take up arms in the defence of their country ; and war could not be proclaimed without the consent of the whole clans in convoca-tion assembled.   It is not, therefore, to be wondered at that ambitious kings, paternally of a foreign and feudal lineage, should strive to substitute the feudal for the patriarchal constitution of Scotland, and that the clans sternly resisted the usurpation. The kings, however, by and by found that, in the feudal nobility, they had created a tyranny which threatened to enslave both the king and the people ; so a change came over the spirit of their dream when it was too late.   While bent on the establishment of the feudal despotism, the king made Mackintosh the captain (not the chief—for each clan had its own chief) of the powerful confederation called Clan Chattan, justiciary of Inverness-shire, for the purpose of reducing into vassalage or extirpating the Macdonells of Braelochaber, the Camerons, and others, who refused to accept feudal charters.   The severity with which Macintosh executed his office is commemorated in an expressive apologetic proverb—*cha ne h-uile la bhithis mōd aig Mac-an-toisich*—*i.e.*, it is not every day Macintosh holds a court.   But when the feudal system was to be put down, Argyle was made justiciary of the Merse, Teviotdale, and the Border districts, and made an incursion there, with the Campbells, which resulted in driving the Douglasses out of Scotland, and breaking the neck of a combination which threatened to destroy all that remained of civil liberty south of the friths.   It was on this memorable occasion that the clan quick-step of "the Campbells are coming" was produced.   The occasion was memorable, and "the Campbells are coming" not unworthy of the achievement.   From this period, until the fall of the dynasty, the Stuart kings fostered the patriarchal, and strove to reduce the feudal power.   Ian Lom, the loyal celtic bard, ascribes to this fact the attachment of the feudal nobility to the revolution party.   He states that their object was so to limit the prerogatives of the king as to secure to themselves unlimited power over the clans, that they might be enabled to give the-same effect to feudal charters in Scotland which they had received in England. They did limit the power of the king, but happily for the country, they were deprived of the feudal jurisdictions (on which the royal despotism had always been some check), and thus frustrated in their object. Charles the First and Second, and James the Seventh, as is instructed by tradition, and that valuable work, the *Memoirs of Lochiel*, became bound to relieve the clans of all the feudal superiorities granted over their estates by their predecessors ; and William the Third, in the treaty concluded at Achchalder by the Earl of Braedalbane, between himself and the clans who were in arms for King James, became also bound to relieve them of these superiorities at the public expense ; but that sublime model of whiggery and orangism seems to have considered afterwards that it would be more easy to extirpate the clans than to buy off the feudal surperiors. Hence the massacre of Glenco, which, according to a rare little work by one of Dundee's officers (which was published in London two or three years after Dundee's death), was only the first act of a tragedy intended to embrace the whole clans concerned in the treaty. King William solemnly ratified the treaty which he had thus violated ; and which remains a dead letter as regards the feudal superiorities until this day.

Logan, the learned author of the *Scottish Gael,*

and other eminent writers of modern times, who quote a host of ancient historians, including Cæsar and Tacitus, shew that the Celts were the earliest known inhabitants of Europe. They consisted of innumerable clans, and formed separate states and confederations; but every clan was self-governed, and lived in what Chalmers, in his *Caledonia,* describes as a state of disunited independence. The scattered and isolated positions of the different clans involved such a variety of climates and pursuits, and such vicissitudes in circumstances and modes of life, as to produce different manners and customs, and even different dialects and costumes among the different states and confederations. Hence, in the course of ages, the opinion prevailed that they were descended from different races, and had emigrated to Europe, from the cradle of mankind in the East, at different ages. The original common name of the whole race was the Gael; but as descriptive names accorded with their customs and the genius of their language, I think the proper spelling is *Geal,* white, in contradistinction to the variously coloured races of the east. It was spelt in different ways by the Greeks—Celtae, Calatae, Galatae, Galli, Gallatians, Gaul—but the etymon, according to Greek scholars, is Galactori, that is, milky-coloured. Some writers who hold that there was a second emigration into Europe of tribes from the East, contend that the latter were of a different and a superior race ; but they have not, as yet, condescended to trace this favourite race to any new act of creative power—nay, they have not even given them a name implying a common mother-country, or a common ancestry. On the contrary, the names by which the different clans became known to their panegyrists do indicate a common origin, being merely local territorial names. Dacia on the Danube, gave their names to the Daces, Getia to the Getes, Moesia to the Moesa, &c., &c. Although their very names thus prove the European origin of these tribes, a vast amount of ingenuity has been expended in fruitless attempts to trace them to a new emigration from the East, and hence to the settlement of a different race from their Celtic predecessors, in the localities from which their clan names are derived.

Roman historians allege that the Celtic clans were quarrelsome, and continually at war with one another ; but their accuracy, when writing of their " barbarian" neighbours, admits of some doubt. The same may be said of the feudal writers of the lowlands and England, who give a similar character of the highland clans. Yet I have never been able to discover any grounds for these allegations. Until feudal despotism had set mankind by the ears, the Celtic clans were a peaceful, kindly, social people. Indeed, all the battles known to tradition as fought between highland clans, originated in the grant by some usurping power of a superiority to some chief or lord over the lands of some independent clan or branch of a clan. These iniquitous grants were always resisted, and gave rise to many *feuds*, a name which sufficiently explains the source whence they sprang. In the letter of the people of Scotland to the Pope, in the days of Wallace, they give the most unqualified contradiction to the interested reports of their internal quarrels made to him by their enemies. Indeed, the patriarchal clans were proverbially friendly and hospitable, which certainly infers the very reverse of the greediness and churlishness of disposition which have ever been the characteristics of the grasping and the aggressive. Add to these facts, that chiefships were elective, that the lands belonged to the clans in common, and that they had thus neither the despotic organisation necessary to military enterprise, nor motives of sufficient strength to excite them to aggressive conflicts and civil warfare. In short, the patriarchal system was only adapted for a peaceful or defensive state of society. It was not until the Romans initiated among the Germans a despotic organisation that the Celtic clans became transformed into the Gothic, and entered on a career of conquest and spoliation. Feudalism, here referred to, was the invention of the emperor Alexander Severus, who hired a number of German clans, by making them grants of land along his frontier on the Danube, on the express condition of their becoming his feudal vassals, and serving him in his wars. This is the first and earliest notice of feudal tenures I have been able to discover in Europe. For Cæsar informs us that clanship existed in Germany, but neither a chief nor any other person had any estate or defined portion of the land; and Tacitus, who wrote a hundred years after Cæsar, states that among the Germans the land was occupied by the whole people of the different tribes in common. Now, the Germany of Cæsar and Tacitus included almost the whole countries occupied by the clans arbitrarily called Teutons or Goths. It extended from the Rhine to the Vistula, and southward to the country of the Scythians and Sarmatians, now called Russia and Tartary. It was bounded by the sea on the north, and the Danube on the south, so that it comprehended (exclusive of what is now called Germany) Bohemia, Hungary, Holland, and Poland, and the countries of Denmark, Norway, Sweden, and Finland.

The whole clans occupying these countries down to the age of feudalism, possessed the lands in common, according to both Cæsar and Tacitus; and they elected their own judges, chiefs, chieftains and kings; or, more properly speaking, CEANN-CATHs or war-chiefs; but so infectious is the desire of individual wealth and power, that within two centuries after the initiation of feudalism into

Germany, a host of popular leaders started up
among the hitherto orderly and peaceable Celtic
clans, who hoisted the banner of aggression and
spoliation. These fierce leaders readily found,
among their warlike countrymen, hundreds of
thousands who enlisted under them, in feudal
vassalages, for the conquest and partition of the
Roman empire. The superinduction of the feudalism
thus introduced, on the system of disunited independence of the Celtic clans, as already stated, made,
in the course of ages, such a change in their districts,
manners, and customs as, in the absence of records,
led many acute and able writers to believe that a
new emigration, and a different and a superior race of
men had come from the east to Europe, and conquered
and expelled the ancient Celtic nations. Yet it is
admitted on all sides, by the disputants in reference
to this unaccountable emigration, that it only took
place about a century before the Christian era, and
that the whole countries taken possession of by these
so-called Gothic clans were previously occupied by
Celts. Now, I think it is impossible to believe
that so vast and violent a change as the immigration of millions of Gothic clans, and the conquest
and expulsion of millions of Celts, could have taken
place in Europe, a century before the Christian era,
without being noticed by both Greek and Roman
historians. Yet we look in vain in their works for
any account of the arrival of the Goths in Europe,

and the conquest and expulsion of the Celts. In short, as Chalmers, who believed in this imaginary immigration, conquest, and expulsion, is forced to admit, " we have really not a vestige of evidence of such immigration." Nevertheless, this stickler for authorities, and who also refers to the *mutability* of language, holds that language is decisive on the question of this alleged immigration. " On this event," he says, "history is silent, but philology is instructive." His intuitive honesty, however, apparently struggled against this preconceived opinion ; for he demolishes the argument founded on language in the very next sentence, by coming out with the great fact (ignorance of which has mis-led historians for more than a thousand years), namely, that " the Gothic is certainly derived from a common origin with the most ancient languages of the European world—the Greek, the Latin, and the *Celtic.*" We have here the true explanation of the error that has so confounded and wrapped in darkness the pedigree of the whole peoples of Europe for upwards of a thousand years—the assumption that the Gothic dialects of Europe, instead of being dialects of the mother language of Europe, which resulted from the comparative isolation of the different clans, and the loose pronunciation and spelling of the dark ages, are the separate and distinct dialects of separate and distinct races of men.

" There can be no doubt," says the learned and philosophic Logan, " that local position, commerce, and other circumstances will, in process of time, occasion so much difference between branches of an original race as to make them appear, in the course of time, like different nations." Thucydides informs us that, before the time of Homer, there was no difference between the Greeks and " barbarians." Homer's works, which, no doubt, were extensively rehearsed and copied into innumerable manuscripts, and the close intercourse among the Greeks, tended to fix their language ; while the scattered positions, in comparatively isolated districts, of the Gothic nations, and the non-existence among them of learned orders, like the Druids, whose bards and seannachies took especial care to carry down from age to age, in their purity and integrity, the poetry and tales which constituted Celtic literature, caused such a continual change in Gothic dialects, as at length to furnish every clan and nation of them with a separate dialect. The Greek and Gothic have a common origin ; and the Latin can be more easily traced to the Gaelic of the Umbri—the ancient inhabitants of Italy—than the modern English can be traced to the Anglo-Saxon. According to the Gunluag Saga, an Englishman and a Northman could converse with one another in the tenth century, without the one being able to discover, by his language, that the other was a foreigner ; yet the

English and the Norse differ more at this day than the Gothic or Earse of Ireland from the ancient Anglo-Saxon. The change in habits and circumstances, and the difference between the peoples of different countries in scientific, manufacturing, and commercial pursuits, accounts for every difference between these different peoples— differences which ignorance and prejudice ascribe to an imaginary difference of race. So great is the difference, for instance, between modern English and Anglo-Saxon, that I have no doubt the editors of the Irish Ossian might have mixed up Anglo-Saxon poetry, properly spelt, with his verses without the one being known from the other by the great majority of their readers. I am convinced that an Irish scholar can understand Anglo-Saxon better than any English scholar. Why, Bosworth, who fancied that he understood the Saxon chronicles, uses more than five words of English for every three words of Anglo-Saxon in his imaginary translations. Had the Anglo-Saxon been so written as to preserve the initial letter of the monosyllables, like the Earse or Gothic of the south of Ireland, an Irish scholar could have no difficulty in reading the Saxon chronicles: at least, I am convinced that an Irish or Gaelic scholar can read them better than any person who has no knowledge of these dialects. Magnusen, a learned Northman, quoted by Sir John Sinclair, informs us that the

Fingalians and the Northmen might have conversed with one or other without an interpreter; **and** Tacitus states that the Gothic and Celtic were merely dialects of the same language ; and that the Cimbri and the Estii, two Belgic tribes, spoke the British dialect. Every scholar knows that south Britain, at the date of the Roman invasion, contained at least as many of the so-called Belgæ and Saxons as of Celts ; yet Cæsar states that, in religion, language, manners, and customs, the inhabitants were like the Gauls. A learned antiquary, Mr Laing, travelled in the north, Denmark, Norway, and Sweden, a few years ago, and came to the conclusion that all these countries were first occupied by the Celts, the whole names of mountains, rivers, &c., being only significant in Gaelic. He accordingly fell into the views of the beaten-track historians, and concluded that the original inhabitants had been conquered and expelled by the Goths. He found nothing to lead him to the conclusion that wars and violence had been the medium of effecting so great a change ; and he knew the rapidity with which language changed among an illiterate people, before printing was known and books published. Yet, from the influence of pre-impressions, he found it more easy to believe that the brave, fiery, and tenacious Celt had tamely yielded to his Gothic invader, and abandoned his country without striking a blow in the defence of his families and hearth, than to come to the simple and natural conclusion that the modern greatly differs from the ancient language of the north of Europe. Chalmers fell into the same error with Laing, and from the same cause—namely, the perverting influence of pre-impressions. He continued to believe that the ancient Celts and Goths were of different races, while adducing reasons, and quoting facts, which prove the reverse. He tells us, for instance, that the shields of the Caledonians and Germans were small and circular ; and he regards the fact as a pendicle of evidence, shewing that the Caledonians were of German lineage. He also tells us that the Scythians and Scots used large oblong shields ; but, pre-impressed with the opinion that the Scots were of the Celtic, and the Scyths of the Gothic race, he does not see in the peculiarity of their shields any reason for concluding that the Scyths and Scots are of the same lineage. Now, had he taken as much pains to ascertain the etymon of Scuit and Scyth as he has taken with that of less important names, he would have found that both are Gothic names for a shield, and would, in all probability, have been thus led to the conclusion that both clans were of Gothic descent, and owe their names to their peculiarly-shaped shields. *Sgia* is the Gaelic name for a wing, and also for a shield ; *ti* for a great being or hero, and *ain* is the plural affix. Now, the *g* and *c* and the *i* and *y* were convertible letters among the Goths. Hence Scythian

is the Gothic of Sgia-thi-ain, the heroes of the shield.
And Bosworth shews that Scuit occurs thus in the
first Anglo-Saxon version of the Lord's prayer—
" Oc Scuit os fra ibel." In the second oldest version, Scuit is made "seld us frae ibel ;" and in a
still more recent translation, it becomes " shield us
from evil." Whoever qualifies himself to analyse
the Gothic dialects, will find the roots of every one
of them in the Celtic.*

* Happening to be in a company in Glasgow when the conversation turned on the above subject, and to have Bosworth's Anglo-
Saxon Grammar, which I had just borrowed from a friend, in my
possession, I offered to convince the gentlemen present that the so-
called Anglo-Saxon was merely Gaelic vulgarly pronounced, and
taken down from the ear. The Rev. Mr Logan, a clergyman then
living in the neighbourhood of Glasgow, took down from Bosworth's
Anglo-Saxon the words, and the translation of them, marked in
the first and second columns, and I gave offhand the Gaelic equiva-
lents, as marked in the third column.

Anglo-Saxon.	English.	Gaelic.
Ganra,	a goose,	ganradh (dh silent).
Clugga,	bells,	cluig.
Sona,	heroes,	soun, a hero ; suin, heroes.
Ean,	a river,	abhainn (bh pronounced v).
Heretoah,	a leader,	fear-toisich, a leader.
Scir,	a county,	sgir, a parish.
Mader,	mother,	mathair (th aspirated).
Boga,	a bow,	boghadh (the gh and dh silent).
Saga,	laws,	laghadh (gh aspirated, dh silent).
Spora,	spurs,	sporadh (dh silent).
Wig,	a recess,	uig.
Uige,	mind,	aigne.
Dal,	part, or portion,	stial.
Gidale,	a croft,	gedeag.
Freo,	a freeman, or root,	freamh (mh silent).
Deor,	a dwarf,	deorl.

The confederations of the Gothic, as well as the Celtic clans, used to elect their kings, or more properly ceann-caths or war-chiefs, from each clan in succession ; and the confederation took the name of the ceann-caths for his life-time. This was well known to the ancient bards and seannachies, and to Greek and Roman historians, who, in like manner. called their armies by the name of the leaders ; but it seems to have wholly escaped the singularly ill-qualified historians of Scotland and Ireland. Hence Ireland is represented as invaded and conquered by countless nations, who, in the history of Ireland, came and disappeared in the most puzzling man-ner ; when the whole matter was the mere succes-sion of one ceann-cath, who gave his name to the confederation, to an other ceann-cath, whose name, of course, disappeared on his death. Thus the Belgæ appeared and disappeared at different periods, in a manner unaccountable to Irish historians. It was the same case with the Scuit, &c., who appeared as the ruling clan in Irish history, several centuries before the Christian era, and then disappeared until

Anglo-Saxon.	English.	Gaelic.
Ric,	a kingdom,	rioghachd (gk aspirated, ac gut-teral, hd silent).
Wen,	a woman,	ben.
Dun,	a knoll,	dun.
Duna,	knolls,	dunadh (dh silent .
Wiln,	a girl,	cailean.
Wilna,	girls,	caileagan.
Fisc,	fish,	iasg.
Fisca,	fishes,	iasgadh (dh silent,.

they gave a new ceann-cath to the Irish clans after the death of Cathmor. Ossian is the best historian of the Irish events of which he treats ; nor are his brief and graphic sketches incapable of corroboration. Saint Benean, in the *Book of Rights*, Dr Lynch, in his *Cambrensis Eversus*, and others, in many works of undoubted authority, recently published by the Archæological and Ossianic Societies of Ireland, and *which could not have been known to Macpherson*, shew that his "fabrications" are substantially true. They distinctly shew, for instance, that Cairber and Oscar MacOiscin killed one another at Gabhra, near Tara. They also shew that Cathairmor, the Cathmor of Ossian, was killed in a few days afterwards by the Fein (the Fingalians of Ossian), in the battle of Tailten (the Temora of Ossian). The leading incidents of Ossian's Temora, one of Macpherson's grossest fabrications, are thus proved to be facts by works recently brought to light, and published by learned societies of Irish gentlemen. I must remark here, with regret, that the editors of some of these works had the bad taste to brand the translator of the venerable Celtic bard as a forger of the very poems to whose historical accuracy these very works bear testimony. The war between the Gothic clans of the south, and the Celtic clans of the north of Ireland, has left indelible traces in the topography of Ireland ; and the march that divided the territories of the one from those

of the other, is one of the most prominent landmarks at this day in Ireland. Yet, these learned
antiquaries prefer silly fables about an Irish militia
(the existence of which was not only inconsistent with,
but impossible under either the patriarchal or the
feudal institutions), to illustrating the genuine antiquities of their country. I am satisfied that the
Erimonians, the Firbolg, or Belgians, the Scuit, &c.,
&c., were different Gothic clans in the south of
Ireland ; and that the Cruithne, Picti, Tutha-de-
danans, &c., &c., were different Celtic clans in the
north-west of Ireland. Saint Benan tells us that
every tribe paid a fixed tribute, in cattle, &c., to the
King of Caishel, *excepting when its own chief was
King of Caishel.* This confirms my statement that
the chief of every clan became ceann-cath in turn,
and was then called King of Caishel for life. Hence
the tribe whose chief was King of Caishel became
the ruling tribe, and gave their name to the confederation. Saint Benan, in the *Book of Rights*, Dr
Lynch in *Cambrensis Eversus*, and other Irish writers,
state that the Brehon laws of Ireland were written
in the *Feinean* (Fingalian) language ; that they
were translated into Latin by a Monk of Iona ; and
from his Latin into Saxon by King Alfred (under the
name of the Malmuta laws of Ireland). Columba,
who was a Scot, employed an interpreter in his
interview with the King of the Caledonians, and the
Albanic Duan, repeated by a Scot at the coronation

of Malcolm the Third is in the *Earse* or Gothic of Ireland, and an entirely different dialect from that of the Caledonian bards, whether of ancient or modern times. There can be no doubt that the language of the Fein and their allies, the Cruithne, Picti, Tuadh-dhaoine (Tuatha-de-danans of the Irish), &c., spoke a different dialect from the southern clans of Ireland; and there can be as little doubt that the Caledonians and Scots also spoke different dialects. The question, therefore, is, whether it was the Caledonians or Scots that were Celtic?

In the wars between England and Scotland, from the earliest period down to the union, we find that the army of the latter country, according to the uniform testimony of English historians, consisted of two different races, whom these historians distinguish from one another by the names of Scots and Red-shanks. No one can doubt that the high-landers in their kilts and tartan hose, were those called Red-shanks; but whence came the Scots? Were they a myth, or the veritable people known as the lowlanders, who seem to be so sadly ignorant of their war-like Scottish descent, as to feel apparently very grateful to the penny-a-liners for having com-passionated and provided for them a species of piebald Anglo-Saxon pedigree?

The colony of Dalriada, which I will call Attacotti (northern Scots), to distinguish them from the great and numerous Gothic clans, in their mother country (who assumed the name of Scots, when the chief of that tribe became ceann-cath, after Cathair-mor was killed by Fingal), may be regarded as the advanced post in Britain of that confederation. These clans, immediately after the battle of Tailten or Temora, first planted a colony in Ulster, and another, shortly after, under the same leader, in Kintyre. It seems very uncertain whether these settlements, especially that of Kintyre, were the result of conquest or of a friendly treaty. Ossian, whom I regard as the best authority on any subject embraced by his poems, shews very clearly in his poem of Temora, that although Fingal gained "the last of his battles," his army was reduced to the last extremity. He had not a single leader of distinction left, excepting Ossian, to whom he delivered his spear on that fatal field ; and his allies, the northern clans of Ireland, were evidently in no better condition. The probability, therefore, certainly is, that the new ceann-cath of the Gothic clans of Ireland, followed up the fatal battle of Tailten or Temora by first invading Ulster, and then Kintyre, and planting a colony in each. This presumption is countenanced, if not confirmed, by fragments of poetry in which Ossian touchingly laments the degeneracy of his people, and taunts them as "the sons of little men." At the same time, if I am right in assuming that the Gaelic and Gothic were cognate dialects, differing more in pronunciation and spelling than in roots or mono-

syllables, both settlements were matters of treaty—
for *dal* means a part or portion, and *reite* means
concord or peace.   Now, both settlements or colonies
were called Dalriada, which, spelt by a Gael, would
be Dal-reite, the portion of concord or peace.   Hence,
Eochaid, who founded these colonies, was, according
to Bede, called Eochaid Riada or Reuda, which, in
my opinion, should be Eochaid-na-reite, for I am
inclined to believe that Eochaid got the addition to
his name from some treaty of peace, and Bede distinctly states that Eochaid had entered into a treaty
with the Caledonians on settling in Kintyre.   And
Pinkerton is certainly wrong in saying that it was
"customary" to call localities by the names of
individuals, and that Dalriada or Reuda was so-called
after "Eochaid Riada or Reuda."   On the contrary,
all local territorial names, with rare and memorable
exceptions, like the above, were descriptive ; but
the names or titles of individuals, and even tribes,
as is shewn by the names of the Gothic tribes
formerly mentioned, were taken from local territorial
names.

The Irish (Goths), according to Mr G. Kearney,
editor of a book containing a stupid burlesque on
Ossian's poem of Temora, called *Cath Garbha*,
published by the Ossianic Society of Dublin, wore
tartans and broad blue bonnets ; and both Chalmers
and Pinkerton, without meaning to do so, make
quotations, which shew that wearing the *breaca*

(instead of the kilt, I presume, which was regarded as a mere "rag wrapped round the loins" and not worth mentioning), was the great distinction between clans (and not dialects) in ancient times. The Irish mantle, to which Spenser shews such antipathy, in a valuable little work published by him on his return from Ireland in the reign of Queen Elizabeth, was simply the double plaid, universally worn by the Scots lowlanders, and still worn by shepherds, which was folded round the body and fastened on the breast with a broach or pin. The Gothic Irish, like the lowland Scots, also wore trews instead of kilts, or "a rag wrapped round their loins." Mr G. Kearney states, on the authority of the *Book of Fermoy*, that the Fein (and no doubt the Caledonians of the north of Ireland, although he does not say so), on the contrary, wore "a dress exactly similar to that of the modern highlanders." In short, it is impossible to read Chalmers, Pinkerton, Logan, Lowe (and the passages they quote), and the works recently published by learned societies in Ireland, without being convinced that the Scots, Belgs, &c., &c., of the south of Ireland were of the Gothic race, and that the Fein, Cruithne, Picti, &c., &c., of the north of Ireland, were Celtic. The Caledonians and Scots were distinguished from each other by the kilt and trews down to the days of Wallace. For Blind Harry, the historian of the patriot-hero, in describing the interview between himself and the Mayor of Perth, makes the latter speak thus:

> The Mayor said, Sir, I speir it for none ill,
> But fell tidings is brought us till,
> Of ane Wallace, was born in the west,
> Our kingsmen he holds in great unrest ;
> Martyrs them down, great pity is to see—
> Out of the *trews* I trow he be.

As the lowlanders, or *trews* men, were inclined to submit to the invader, and live in peace, the mayor very naturally seems to have concluded that Wallace was one of the wild kilted warriors, who kept the "kingsmen in unrest." "*Out* of the *trews* I trow he be," concludes the peace-loving mayor; and the tradition in the highlands certainly is, that Wallace was not a Scot, but a Walense Briton, and wore the kilt ; which, very probably, was the dress of the Walenses or Britons of Strathclyde (Wallace's clan), as well as that of the Caledonians of former ages.

That Ireland was called Scotia or Scotland ages before Eochaid and the Attacotti crossed the Irish Channel, is beyond all doubt. Nor has it ever been shewn, on any other than the most questionable authority, that they had ever been in Scotland until long after they were known to have been the ruling clan in Ireland. *Land* is certainly not a Gaelic, but it is a Scottish word ; and the king of the people that gave the name of Scotland to the lowlands, styled himself King of Scots. The Caledonians never knew their country, on the contrary, by any other name than Albion or Albin. The name, Scotland, therefore, identifies the king and his Scots with the Gothic races of England and Ireland, in the same manner in which Albion and Albin identifies the Caledonians with the Cambrians of Wales, or the northern clans of Erin. At the same time, I am satisfied, as already stated, that there was no difference of race between the Celts and Goths. Indeed, the more recent and able writers on the subject have shewn that the Persians, the Greeks, the Italians, the Goths, the Sclavonians, the Franks, and the Celts, are all of the family called the Argan Family of India, all branches of one and the same people. But be that as it may, the lowlanders of Scotland, and the people of the south of Ireland, are evidently descended from the same race who were at war with the Fein and the northern clans of Ireland. Hence both the southern Irish and the lowlanders of Scotland, equally inherited, and have shewn their hostility to Ossian, in the most fraternal and unique manner—namely, by writing innumerable parodies and burlesques in ridicule of his heroes. But the most singular and amusing thing is, that the Ossianic Society of Dublin is collecting, with great industry, and publishing at great expense, these pasquinades, as genuine remains of the great Celtic bard himself—

and that too, strange to say, for the *honour* of old
Ireland! They are certainly muniments of the
humorous and satirical genius of the descendants of
the Gothic clans, who had been at war with the
Celtic clans and their Fenian allies, when understood
as burlesques on Ossians panegyrics on the Finga·
lians ; but the nationality that can regard them as
an *honour* in any other sense, cannot certainly be
appreciated out of Ireland. The ludicrous figure
which the following verse makes of Fingal, whose
every act, in the poems of Ossian, is that of the hero
and the patriot, and whose every sentence was that
of the philanthropist and the gentleman, shews that
it was never written by a friend. The hills named
in the verse, tower on either side of the valley of
Lubar :

> With one foot on Cromlec's brow,
> The other on Cromell the dark,
> Fion could bale (out) with his large *paw*,
> The vale of Lubar of many waters.

In Mr O'Kearney's translation of the Irish burlesque
on Temora, which he calls by the sounding name of
Cathgarbha, the following are to be found in ridicule
of Oscar, among many equally extravagant in reference to other Feinean leaders. How any society of
educated gentlemen could allow the grotesque
rhapsodies of the moon-struck lunatic (that could
write such verses as the following) to be published

as genuine remains of Ossian, is incomprehensible to me :

The men of Eire hearkened,
Although the cessation was painful,
To the sound of the strokes
That passed between the two Oscars.

As many as two score shields,
In each contending struggle,
MacGarraidh the fierce, and my own son,
Broke in the battle of Gabhra. ·

There were four-and-twenty wounds
On the skin of Oscar, from the struggle;
When retiring from the forces of Cairbre,
To the standard of MacGarraidh.

There were on the skin of MacGarraidh,
When retiring from the battalions of Oscar,
Six-score gaping wounds ;
Were not the Oscars brave ?

Three showers arose
Over their heads in the strife—
A shower of blood, a shower of fire,
And a bright shower from their shields.

MacGarraidh was worsted,
Though the task was difficult,
By Oscar, who never failed
In liberality to the learned.

Nor failed my son,
Whose career was never impeded ;
He drove the nimble javelin
To the cross through Cairbre.

Until the grass of the plain is numbered,
And every grain of sand of the sea-coast,
All who fell by my son,
Cannot possibly be numbered.

The anachronisms, in these clumsy satires on Ossian, shew that they were composed in the dark ages of spiritual and feudal despotism, when Roman Catholic heroes, including even the heathen Fingal, went on pilgrimages to Rome, and when the Lords of the Pale exacted the *mulier mercata* for consenting to the marriage of the daughters of their vassals and serfs. The lowlanders have shewn themselves less extravagant in their burlesques, but not one iota less hostile to Ossian's poems and heroes than their Gothenian brethren in Ireland. Indeed, while the kings of the Scots and their lowland vassals were struggling to impose the feudal yoke on the stubborn necks of the highland clans, every lowland bard of any note had a kick at Ossian's poems and heroes. I quoted many of these, in my articles on Ossian, in the *West of Scotland Magazine;* but beg leave to quote here also two short verses as specimens of the animus by which they were inspired. The following verses from Allan Ramsay's *Evergreen,* seems to have been written in ridicule of the stature of Gaul:

> My fader, mucle Gow MacMorm,
> That frae his moder's wame was shorne,
> For littleness was too forlorn,
> Siccan a kemp to bear.

Ridicule of the deeds ascribed to Fingal was evidently the object of the following couplet:

> My grandsire hicht Fin MacCoul,
> Wha dang the deil and gart him youl.

In short, it can be shewn that the descendants of the southern or Gothic clans, who had been at war with the northern or Celtic clans of Ireland, and their Fenian allies, both in Ireland and Scotland, composed innumerable parodies and burlesques in ridicule of Ossian's poems and heroes, in the south of Ireland and Scotland; while the bards of the north of Ireland and the north of Scotland refer to them in thousands of verses, which are still extant, and cannot be regarded otherwise than poetic, feeling, and beautiful. I think these facts form no slight pendicle of the evidence proving that the clans of the south of Ireland and the south of Scotland were of the Gothic, and those of the north of Ireland and the north of Scotland, of the Celtic race.

Eochaid, who placed the Attacotti in Kintyre, entered into a treaty with the Caledonians, and they and the Belgæ or Saxons made several foraging expeditions into the Roman province, until they acquired a knowledge of the strongholds, numbers, and tactics of the enemy, and a confidence in one another. They seem, then, to have determined on the conquest and division of the province among them. With this view, they renewed the original treaty, or entered into a new one, as we are told both by Bede and Eumenius. This occurred in 296. Some may consider this preliminary step to the invasion and conquest of the Roman province, as by much too enlightened a piece of diplomacy on the part of "the naked and painted Caledonians," and their Scottish allies; and so much are we accustomed to follow the beaten track of history, without questioning the accuracy of those by whom it was made, as scarcely to justify me in expecting that you will listen to my views on the subject otherwise than with incredulity. Yet I am perfectly satisfied, if you can emancipate your minds from pre-impressions, and judge from the facts stated, instead of the opinions expressed on hearsay, by ancient historians, that you will find enough to corroborate my statements, or at least to make you doubt what is inconsistent in the statements of foreign writers, in reference to the condition of the Caledonians. For instance, Tacitus states that the inland seas of Britain were so stagnant and thick that it was difficult to impel ships through them, either with sails or oars; and another historian, Procopius, says that there was a province of Britain where the ground was covered with serpents, and that to breathe its air was death. He says the spirits of the Franks were carried over there at night by fishermen; and that these fishermen could hear the howling of the ghosts, wandering on their ghostly rounds through these dismal territories, as they approached its shores. Yet with such evidence of the credulity and inaccuracy of ancient historians, we believe whatever they say as to the utter barbarity of our ancestors! The Caledonians were in the habit of stripping to the kilt before going into battle, and of painting their crests on their naked breasts, so as their bodies might be recognised, and receive funeral honours (on which, previously to the introduction of Christianity, they placed a religious value) from their friends. Hence the Romans, and even the feudal writers of the lowlands and England, writing chiefly from hearsay, and regarding or representing the kilt as a mere "rag wrapped round the loins," speak of the army of Galgacus as *naked* and *painted* savages; and of the army of Claverhouse as *naked* savages. Yet the army of Galgacus had swords, daggers, targets, standards, spears, and chariots, which is utterly inconsistent with the statement that they were naked and painted savages; and the army of Claverhouse was certainly neither more naked nor more savage than the highland regiments of the present day ; although the free and rapid action, and " *eireachdas lann*" (the beautiful play of swords), in which the clans delighted, made them strip to the kilt, also before going into the battle of Killiecrankie. The poetry, tales, and traditions of the highland clans, furnish abundant materials to refute the absurd and contradictory statements that represent the ancient highlanders as a barbarous race; and until their calumniators qualify themselves to peruse these, there is a degree of recklessness in their hap-hazard repetitions of ancient errors on the subject, which is altogether inconsistent with the love of truth, and the propriety of thought, which usually characterise literary gentlemen.

The treaties, necessary to their unity and success, being concluded between the Caledonians and Scots. the former, advancing from the north, stormed and carried the wall between the Forth and Clyde, while the latter, crossing the channel in their currachs, turned their left flank and threatened their rear. A terrible weapon, which, from its effects, seems to have been the Lochaber axe, was used by the Caledonians on this occasion with deadly success.

For the defenders of the wall are described as cut
down on the rampart, or hooked and dragged head-
long into the fosse by this merciless implement.
The intrepid allies having carried the wall, pursued
their victorious career to the south, killed the
Roman governor and admiral, who tried to impede
their progress, and not only conquered the district,
which was afterwards called Valentia, but even
stormed the southern wall, and overran both Wales
and England. The Saxons are named as joined to
the Caledonians and Scots in more than one of
their foraging expeditions, which shews that there
were Saxons in Britain long before the Romans
voluntarily (as their admirers assert) left the
country. Indeed Kemble, the most recent if not
the most able historian on the subject of the Anglo-
Saxons, treats the story of Hingest and Horsa, the
Saxon princes, who made a dotard of old Vorti-
gern, and the army of mercenaries who conquered
the Britons " by a glorious massacre," as baseless
fabrications. Many so-called Gothic clans, of whom
the Saxons were probably a tribe, occupied the
whole plains and shores of south Britain ages before
Cæsar crossed the British channel.

Theodocius, who was despatched to drive the
Caledonians and Scots out of the Roman province,
must have considered these daring invaders as
something very different from the naked and painted
savages described by the credulous historians of

the Romans, else he scarcely could have deemed it necessary to reinforce the Roman and provincial troops still in the country, numbering about thirty thousand, with about seventy thousand additional troops. And it would appear that even the sight of this formidable array of well-armed and disciplined troops, under the most illustrious leader of the age. did not scare these unorganised and undrilled barbarians, like deer, into their native covers. On the contrary, they offered and gave battle to this enormous army, but were defeated with a slaughter—which seems to have fallen chiefly on the Hiberni—a slaughter which, according to the panegyrist, spread lamentations and dismay all over icy Irne. The Scots are described as driven over the Hyperborean Sea, and the Caledonians into Thule ; but our Scottish historians, unwilling, apparently, to give the Hiberni credit for taking any part in driving the Romans out of Britain, deny that the Scots were Hiberni. They also, at the same time, contend that the gulf of Clyde is the Hyperborean Sea, and the river Earne, in Perthshire, the Irne of the Romans ! But they do not condescend to explain why the Attacotti (if they were the only Scots present in the battle) might not have retreated by land to the west, as well as the Caledonians could have retreated by land to the east Highlands. Indeed, the attempt to explain away the undoubted meaning of the Roman panegyrist, in this way, is more characteristic of, than creditable to, Scottish historians.

Theodocius, after his victory, repaired the northern wall, and erected the country between the two walls into a province, which he called Valentia, in compliment to the emperor. He then seems to have assigned that part of this province most exposed to the incursions of the Caledonians, to such of the warlike tribes to whom the country, thus made into a province, originally belonged, as had (unlike the great body of their clansmen) submitted to the Romans. This district became afterwards known as the kingdom of Strathclyde. Theodocius, after having taken the above and other precautions worthy of his reputation, returned to the Continent, in the full belief that he had settled permanently the boundaries of the province, and given their *quietus* to the Caledonians and Scots; but it is not one, nor yet twenty defeats, that ever has or ever will subdue the determination of Caledonian or Scot. We accordingly find, from Claudian and others, that while Valentians and Theodocians were engaged in a war with Maximus, the Scots "moved all Ireland" to join them in the conquest of the Roman provinces. "They had hitherto," says Lowe, "maintained inviolable their treaty with the Caledonians; but beginning to increase in numbers as in power, they determined henceforth to conquer for themselves. They landed in Wales, and conquered the

country of the Demetæ, which included Caer-
marthen, Pembroke, and Cardiganshires ; also
Anglesea, and the Isle of Man ; but they did not
permanently retain these brilliant conquests. While
the Scots were thus fighting to their own hand, the
Caledonians and Saxons were carrying on operations,
with equal success, in Valentia, and even extended
their triumphs beyond the southern wall ; but when
Theodocius became sole emperor, he despatched
Chrysantus to the scene of action, and their career
was checked. " But the effects of the repulses were
short-lived." The Caledonians and Scots again
renewed their alliance, speedily recovered their
reverses, again invaded the provinces, stormed and
carried both walls, and made matters look so despe-
rate as to compel the Romans who had estates in
Britain to sell them and pass over to the Continent. The Caledonians, Scots, and Saxons then
divided the whole country between them, excepting
the district of Strathclyde, which included part of
Dumbarton, and of Lanark, and the whole of Ren-
frewshire. The Caledonians retained the whole
country south of the Frith of Forth between the Catrail and the sea. This singular fosse, with its double
line of ramparts, divided that part of the Roman provinces which was assigned to the Caledonians or Picts,
from those parts of them which were assigned to
the Britons of Strathclyde, and the Scots and
Saxons, is known to the people by the name of the

" Picts-work-ditch." The preservation of this name
affords a striking instance of the manner in which
the traditions of a people can rebuke the historian
who substitutes ingenious conjectures for traditional
facts, when writing of the antiquities of a country
at a period anterior to authentic records. The
traditional name of the Catrail, " Picts-work-ditch,"
sufficiently attests by whom it was made, and its
object—the conjectures of historians and antiquaries,
notwithstanding. It is interesting to remark that a
similar bulwark had been made across Ireland, half-
way between Dublin and Galway, at a still more
early period, to divide the territory of the Firbolg
or Gothic, from that of the Caledonian or Celtic
clans of Ireland. The name Catrail, seems to have
been compounded from the roots *cath*, battle, and
riaghal, pronounced ree-al, to rule, regulate, or
command—a very appropriate name for the boundary line between people whose alliance was, in all
probability, more a matter of policy than cordiality,
and whose warlike propensities required a formidable
line of bulwarks to control and limit aggressive
movements on either side. It was accordingly a
mutually defensive fortification, consisting of a deep
fosse, apparently thirty feet broad, and having a
rampart of twelve feet high, and ten or twelve feet
thick on *each side.* This peculiar feature shews
that it was a *mutual* strength, and intended purely
for mutually defensive purposes. Traces of a simi-

lar work are to be found near Dalmellington ; but I have not had an opportunity of tracing them so far as to enable me to form an opinion of their object ; although I have no doubt that, like the Catrail, they formed the boundary between the Cruithne or Picts of Galloway, and their Briton and Scottish neighbours.

The Catrail began at Penvahl, a name which Chalmers, and other antiquaries, use as an argument in favour of the opinion that the Caledonians or Picts were Gothic, and spoke a Gothic dialect, of which this word, meaning the end of the wall, is regarded as a genuine specimen. I not only admit that it is a genuine specimen, but also a specimen calculated strikingly to illustrate the value that is entitled to be placed on the opinions of writers who affect to find, in dialects of which they do not even know the roots, evidence that all who spake them must have been of different races. The *pen* of the Briton, like the *ceann*, pronounced kén, of the Gael, means an end or a head. Penvahl resolved into its roots, therefore, is *kin* or *pen*, the end, and *balla*, wall. When the two roots are combined into a genuine Gaelic word, they become ceann-bhalla, pronounced kèn-vàhlá. The difference between Penvahl and kèn-vàhlá, may, therefore, be very fairly taken as the measure of the difference between the Celtic and Gothic dialects, as well as the measure of the value of the opinions of writers who find in a

difference of pronunciation and orthography sufficient grounds for distinguishing races.

There appears to be no doubt that the Catrail
began at Penvahl, and divided the territory of the
Caledonians from that of their neighbours, all the
way until it entered the sea near Berwick. I am
not aware that its whole course from Penvahl to
Galashiels has been laid down by any historian or
antiquary; but Chalmers, in his *Caledonia,* to which
I refer, mentions landmarks, such as the names of
ancient forts, hills, moors, rivers, and farms, whereby
it could be traced, in his day, all the way from
Galashiels to Berwick. The Catrail, known best to
the people through whose farms it passes, as the
Picts-work-ditch, extending all the way from Penvahl
to Berwick, and the sea from Berwick to Leith,
were the southern boundaries of the Caledonians, and
an irregular line or ridge called Drimalbin,* literally

* Drimalbin (the back bone of Albin) is a landmark of some
importance in the topography of the country, and some writers—
even eminent writers on the subject—represent it as running east
and west, instead of south and north, through the highlands. It
may be proper to remark that I have followed it above only so far
as it formed the march between the Caledonians and the Britons
of Strathclyde, and the Attacotti, or Scots of Dalriada. From this
point it ran, in an irregular line, along heights and hollows,
between the sources of the waters flowing in different directions,
and thus divided Loch Ranach from Loch Treig, Loch Laggan
from Loch Roy, and Loch Oich from Loch Lochy, at Laggan Achadroma (literally the hollow in the back of Albin). From Laggan

the back of Albin, which stretched in a north-west direction between the sources of the waters that flowed east and west, until it reached the head of Loch Etive, divided Caledonia from the country of the Strathclyde Britons and the Scots. Loch Etive and Loch Linnie were the boundary of Dalriada on the north and east, and the line already described, deviating to the head of Loch Lomond, divided it from Caledonia and Strathclyde.

Lowe, who quotes undoubted authorities most scrupulously for all his statements (which cannot be so conveniently done in lecturing), shews that the possession of the eastern part of Valentia was the subject of a treaty between the Caledonians and Saxons. Indeed, I am satisfied that a more careful investigation of the subject than I have been able to overtake in preparing this paper, would shew that the Caledonians, and Belgæ or Saxons of South Britain, were acting in concert, and with a perfect understanding with one another, in their invasion and partition of the Roman provinces ; and that it was only when the Scots, confiding in their Hibernian strength, shook off the alliance, and began to conquer " for their own hand," that a reinforcement of Saxons were sent for to the continent, not by the Britons, but the British Saxons. Although some

Achadroma, it proceeded, on the same principle, over heights and hollows, dividing the sources of the waters that ran in different directions, until it reached the Deucaledonian sea.

understandings may have afterwards arisen, and some blows been exchanged occasionally, between the Caledonians, Scots, and Saxons, I am convinced, from the period of their first treaty, with the view of conquering and dividing the Roman provinces, that the division to be allotted to each of the allies was agreed upon, and never materially altered until after the conquest of south Britain by the Normans. For, although the King of the Scots ultimately succeeded to the thrones of both the kingdoms of Caledonia and Strathclyde, his civil power was merely nominal, and he neither did alter, or had the power to alter, these boundaries. When the Scots attained such extensive territories south of the Firth of Clyde, I am of opinion that the great body of the Attacotti crossed from Dalriada to Ayrshire; for, from the civil wars and broils in which they were continually involved as to rights of succession, there seems little doubt that the Scots were always under the government of chiefs who had estates and exercised some species of feudal despotism over their clans; but we find that down to the period at which the feudal system was introduced into England by the Normans, and adopted in its fulness and sternness by the King of the Scots, no civil wars or broils, involving questions of succession to estates, prevailed among the clans either of Caledonia or Dalriada.

Before crossing the channel to plant a colony in Kintyre, Eochaid Riada conquered the Cruithne of

Ulster, a warlike tribe, whose Caledonian lineage is attested by their name. When the hands of the Scots were full with their conquests in the Roman provinces, the Cruithne of Ulster not only threw off their yoke, but crossed the channel, and invaded the Scottish possessions in Ayrshire. They suffered a severe defeat at Mauchline from the Scots, supported by the Walensis or Britons of Strathclyde; but succeeded in planting a colony in Galloway, where they maintained their independence for several ages. These Cruithne, or Picts, as they are more generally called, were the men who claimed precedence at the battle of the standard, and shouted Albin! Albin! as their war-cry, and not the Scots. The Caledonian clans, whose chiefs were elective, always took the name of their country, or some favourite locality in their respective clan district, as their war-cries; such for instance as Tullach-ard, Lochsloy, Craigealachie, &c., but the Scots and other Gothic clans, whose chiefs were hereditary and despotic, took their names for their war-cries, as a Piercy, a Stanley, a Douglas, a Darnley, &c., &c. These are marked distinctions, and illustrate the difference between the clansman and vassal, in a manner which the beaten-track writer will find it difficult to explain away.

The conquests of the Scots, according to Lowe (who, as already stated, scrupulously quotes undoubted authorities for all his statements), were greatest beyond the Northumbrian wall. Their first encounter with the united Britons and Saxons was a mere skirmish, and did not check their victorious career. It was not until they reached Stamford, on the border of Rutlandshire, that the United Britons and Saxons, including the new arrivals from the continent, faced them in battle, and put a stop to their further progress southward. The Caledonians or Picts are said, by some writers, to have accompanied the Scots in this expedition; but I am inclined to doubt this (first), because they had, according to Bede and others, entered into a treaty with the Saxons as to the partition of Valentia (as already stated); and (second), because the part of Maxima or Yorkshire that fell to the Picts was so inconsiderable. The Scots retained their conquests to Stamford, forty miles south of Lincoln, and within eighty-eight miles of London. It appears, therefore, that the Scots possessed Northumberland, Durham, York, Lincoln, Nottingham, and Derbyshires, all these being north of Stamford.

Although the Caledonians and Scoto-Irish, as Chalmers very properly calls the Scots and Atticots after they had consolidated their conquest into a kingdom, were only separate families of the same ancient race, they spoke different dialects. Hence Columba, who was a Scot, employed an interpreter in his interview with the King of the Caledonians. The bard who repeated the Albanic Duan, which contained the pedigree of the King of the Scots, at the coronation of Malcolm Ceann-mor, was also a Scot; and yet the Duan is in a decidedly different dialect from that of the contemporary Caledonian bards, as well as from the Gaelic of the present day, which, from the reasons previously explained, has been preserved in its purity from the days of Ossian to the present time. It may be remarked, as an additional proof of the difference between the institutions as well as the dialects of the Caledonians and Scots, that, in the former, we have no words to express the title of either earl, lord, or baronet. Now Malcolm Ceann-mor created earls and lords. Would he have created titles that could only be expressed in a foreign language? And why have the lowlanders no other name for their country excepting Scotia or Scotland, while the Caledonians never had any other name for it excepting Albion or Albin? We have not only no genuine Gaelic words to express titles, but none even to express master and servant. This proves what I have already stated, namely, that with the exception of the elected Brehon or judge, and the chief and chieftains, whose titles and duties have been already explained, the whole clan were on a perfect equality one with another, both in rank and circumstances. Respect to the judge, and to the chief and chieftains, and also to the aged men, and to the women of the clan, was shewn by addressing them in the plural num-

ber, *sibh* (pronounced sheeve), or *sibhse* (pronounced
sheeve-shay), while equals were addressed *u* (oo),
or *usa* (oo-saw). But modern Gaelic grammarians
and lexicographers appear to have had an almost
idolatrous veneration for, and a most magnificent
idea of, dukes and earls, wealth and state. With a
devotion and obsequiousness scarcely paralleled by
the servility of the lower castes of Indians, and totally
inconsistent with the spirit of the Celtic race, and
the genius of the Gaelic language, they borrowed,
eked, and distorted, until they got words to express
every title of exalted rank, or phrase of grovelling
abasement which characterised feudalism. There
might be an amusing volume written in illustration
of the little appreciated labour and ingenuity
exerted by these learned gentlemen to exalt the
higher and degrade the lower classes of highlanders,
for the purpose of shewing that the patriarchal was
the same as the feudal state of society. What do
you think, for instance, of the fertile ingenuity
which suggested that the poverty of the Gaelic in
words to express servitude or a servant-man might
be concealed by combining the monosyllables
og, (ok), young, and *laoch* (law-*och*), a hero,
and calling the compound words a servant man,
in the Gaelic and English dictionary! In like
manner, they combined the feminine root, *og*,
young, and *laoch*, a hero, and represent the
word thus compounded as meaning a servant

woman. It will be admitted that these transforma-
tions were very ingenious, but they were nothing
compared to the effort of genius by which they
concealed the discreditable fact that our idle, lazy,
starving, Celtic ancestors had not a single word in
their language whereby to designate a pauper or
paupers! But the good taste and kindly considera-
tions for the poor of these learned philanthropists
suggested that the name *boc,* a he-goat, would
describe a pauper to a nicety, and that by adding
the plural affix *ibh,* we would have an appropriate
name for paupers! Had our dictionary-makers
reduced the words they quote to their simple elements
or roots, as I have done, to shew the meaning of
these distorted words, instead of following the
example of other lexicographers, and giving a string
of arbitrary meanings to explain that of one word, they
might have furnished us with the means of drawing
such a truthful picture of the thoughts, feelings, and
domestic condition and progress in civilisation of our
ancestors, as would have enabled us to rebuke the
prejudices and ignorance that have represented the
highland clans as grovelling and starving serfs,
living in abject subjection to chiefs and chieftains
as despotic and magnificent as the dukes and lords
of feudal conquerors. The patriarchal institutions
of the Caledonian clans were as free as republi-
canism, and as lofty as aristocracies, and their
dialect was Gaelic; but the institutions of the

Scots were despotic, or a kind of feudalism; for Chalmers clearly shews that they had continual feuds and wars of succession among themselves; which was not the case among the Caledonians, who occupied the soil in common, and were, each clan, self-governed, and living in a state of disunited independence, until the clan system was broken up by the changes consequent on the union with England. Hence the Kings of the Scots, from the date of the conquest of England by the Normans, never ceased to use every means in their power to subject the Caledonian clans to the feudal yoke.

Henry Home, no bad authority, it will be admitted, remarks that, if history or tradition are to be believed, the people of Scotland—Caledonia?—were once a free people. Now, he continues, as it is the plan of the feudal law to bestow the whole land property on the king, and to subject the bulk of the people to him in the quality of servants and vassals —a constitution so contradictory to all the principles which govern mankind can never be brought about " without violence, whether by conquest from without or military force from within." Of violence from without there is no historical evidence. How, then, are we to account for the undoubted fact that the King of the Scots borrowed and ruled his Scots or lowlanders by the feudal laws of England? Scottish lawyers contend for the originality of the feudal law of Scotland; but, I think, not very successfully. The book of Glanville, and the *Regium Majestatem*, are substantially the same ; and it will scarcely be contended that the Normans, who introduced feudal laws into England, borrowed them from Scotland. Henry Home, on the other hand, asserts that " no sooner was a statute passed in England, but, on the first opportunity, it was introduced into Scotland ; so that our oldest statutes are mere copies of those of England." Dempster, who is regarded as one of the best of our antiquaries, states that it was Malcolm the Third who created the first barons and earls in Scotland ; but Chalmers, the author of *Caledonia*, who is equally as good an authority, says that there is not in Scotland a single feudal charter of so early a date as that reign. And certainly we have no author who wrote until many ages after that.

But when we find that the King of the Scots and his peoples borrowed their laws from England, spoke a dialect like the English, and that the lowlanders also strikingly resembled the English in manners and customs, it is scarcely to be wondered at that superficial writers have jumped to the conclusion that the more numerous and powerful people of England had conquered and colonised the lowlands, and driven the Scots beyond the Grampians! But if the lowlanders were Anglo-Saxons, and the highlanders Scots, how is it that the former are uniformly called Red-shanks, and the latter Scots, by the historians of England?   Or if the Anglo-Saxons conquered the lowlands, how is it that they did not attach that district to England, or place a king of their own nation on the throne of Scotland, instead of becoming vassals and serfs to the Scottish king, and allowing him to retain his ancient arms and style of King of the Scots?   That they conquered Scotland, and yet became vassals and serfs to the King of the Scots, is very improbable.   It is also equally improbable that the Scots extirpated the Picts, and took up their residence among the mountains, leaving the great rivers and the rich vales and plains of the lowlands to the English, without striking a blow in their defence.   These assumptions being all extremely improbable, should only be received as facts on very satisfactory historical evidence.   But there is no such evidence; while, not only the whole probabilities, but also the whole historical evidence of the case, prove that the highlanders are the descendants of the Caledonians or Picts, and that the lowlanders are the descendants of the Scots and other Belgic clans.

EDINBURGH : PRINTED BY ALEX. GRANT, 14 ST JAMES' SQUARE.

www.ingramcontent.com/pod-product-compliance
Lightning Source LLC
Chambersburg PA
CBHW022009050726
47499CB00008BA/2730